Daddy Played Music for the Cows

Maryann Weidt
Henri Sorensen

Lothrop, Lee & Shepard Books
New York

Special thanks to Susan Pearson, for listening and hearing a story.
Thank you Tom and Sonja Duesler and Helen and Ray Froemming,
two of our nation's valiant farm families—I salute you!

First Edition   1 2 3 4 5 6 7 8 9 10
Library of Congress Cataloging in Publication Data
Weidt, Maryann N. Daddy played music for the cows / by Maryann Weidt; illustrated by Henri Sorensen.
    p.   cm. Summary: A young girl grows up on a farm to the sound of music from the radio her father plays in the barn.
ISBN 0-688-10057-0. — ISBN 0-688-10058-9 (lib.bdg.) [1. Farm life—Fiction. 2. Music—Fiction.] I. Sorensen, Henri, ill. II. Title.
PZ7.W42575Dad 1996 [Fic]—dc20 94-24576   CIP AC

to my father, Andy Nieberle (1903-1957)
—MW

to my friends for more than 38 years,
Mogens Keblovszki and Palle Isbrandt
—HS

Mama always said I was born in the barn while Daddy played music for the cows. A bright red can full of seed corn was my rattle. It sang *kitch-ka-shoo, kitch-ka-shoo* when I shook it, while the cowboys sang on the radio and Daddy hummed along.

Mama set my playpen in the middle of the barn so I could listen to Daddy play music for the cows. When they strolled inside in slow motion, he picked me up and waltzed me down the aisle between them, patting their wide brown rumps and calling them by name— "Hey, Pearl Bailey, that's my girl....Come on, Queenie....Hello, Dolly"—as he nudged them into place.

The barn cats chased a sunbeam, and the kittens pushed their noses through my playpen bars. I shoved my nose out to meet them, and Daddy squirted warm milk at us while the radio sang *"yo-del-lay-hee-hoo."*

One day the playpen went to the attic, but Daddy still played music for the cows. The chickens danced a two-step in the corner of the barn. I squatted down to see where the eggs came from, and as I watched, out one popped. I caught it with both hands. The shell was soft and brown and warm. When I gave it to Mama, she tucked it into her apron pocket while she sang "Golden Rings" along with the radio.

Sometimes when Daddy played music for the cows, trumpet sounds filled every crack in the barn. Sleeping pigeons looked up from under the eaves. The mourning doves sang *coo-ooh, coo, coo-coo* as they flew down from the rafters, picked bits of corn off the floor, and flew away. I chased after them, laughing, but never caught more than the feathers they dropped.

While Daddy scooped manure from behind each cow, Mama spread hay beneath them. "It's all right, Dolly," she crooned. Dolly nodded and swayed, her hot breath coming in time to the music, as someone on the radio sang about the moon.

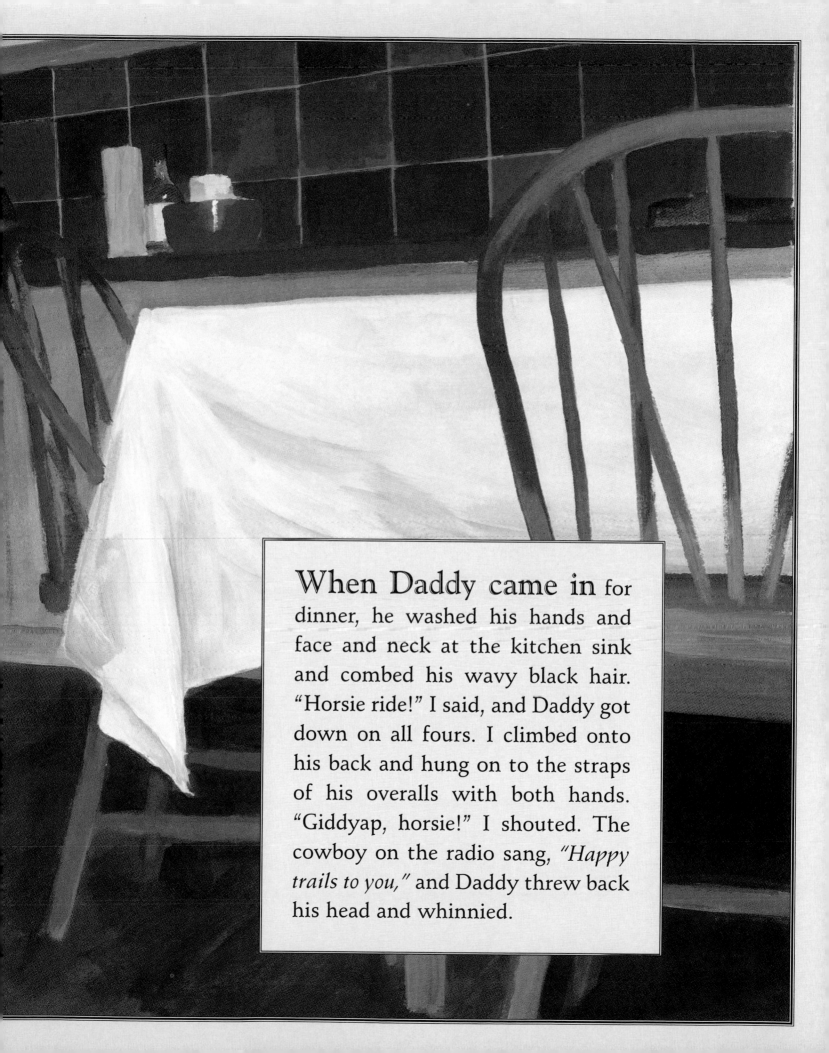

When Daddy came in for dinner, he washed his hands and face and neck at the kitchen sink and combed his wavy black hair. "Horsie ride!" I said, and Daddy got down on all fours. I climbed onto his back and hung on to the straps of his overalls with both hands. "Giddyap, horsie!" I shouted. The cowboy on the radio sang, *"Happy trails to you,"* and Daddy threw back his head and whinnied.

On my first day of first grade, I heard the cowgirls singing as I climbed off the bus and ran up the driveway. I changed my clothes as fast as I could, then raced for the barn. "Daddy!" I shouted. "I can read! Now I have to learn to yodel!"

All that year I listened to the cowgirls and tried to yodel just like them. I yodeled on the school bus. I yodeled when I fetched the cows from the pasture. I whirled and twirled and sang and yodeled and danced the chicken two-step down the center of the barn. *"Yo-del-lay-hee, yo-del-lay-heeee-hoooo."*

In second grade, I worked on my daring circus act. While Mama and Daddy milked the cows, I climbed inside the silo and hung by my knees from the ladder till the smell of silage made me dizzy. Then, holding my nose with one hand, I waved my other to the crowd. Applause bounced up and down the tall, cool walls. A single sunbeam held me in its spotlight while Daddy turned the radio to *"Toe-ray-a-doe-ra!"*

Mama always told me, "Don't play in the haymow," but when Jackie Bonniwell dared me, I climbed to the top, grabbed the rope, and swung like Tarzan across the whole length of the barn. When I let go, I fell screaming into a feather bed of hay. I felt like I was tumbling along with the tumbling tumbleweeds.

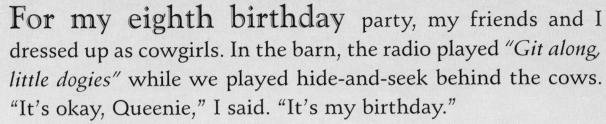

For my eighth birthday party, my friends and I dressed up as cowgirls. In the barn, the radio played *"Git along, little dogies"* while we played hide-and-seek behind the cows. "It's okay, Queenie," I said. "It's my birthday."

When Mama called, "Cake and ice cream!" we joined arms, kicked our boots in the air, and danced across the yard, singing *"Whoopee ti-yi-yo."*

When I was as tall as Daddy's armpit, I climbed onto the tractor and he showed me which levers to push and which to pull. Then I drove the tractor while Daddy and Mr. Bonniwell and Jackie put up hay. We worked all day and into the night to get the hay up before the rain. The music in my head sang one song after another: *Toe-ray-a-doe-ra...Happy trails to you...Yo-del-lay-hee-hooooooo.*

"Run and get the cows," said Daddy when the last load of hay was in the barn. I slid down the path to where Dolly and Pearl and Queenie were waiting with the others. I patted their soft warm bellies. Then, as they followed me to the barn, I lifted my chin and sang to the raindrops.

Daddy hugged me and laughed. "You look like a wet little muskrat," he said, "just like the day you were born." The air smelled of wet cows and steaming manure. "Listen," said Daddy as he turned up the radio. A cowgirl was singing our favorite song. Daddy hummed along, his voice flat and happy, and I yodeled like I never had before, while Daddy played music for the cows.

ANIMAL KINGDOM CLASSIFICATION

NEMATODES, LEECHES & OTHER
WORMS

By Steve Parker

Content Adviser: Leonard Muscatine, Ph.D.,
Emeritus Professor of Biology
University of California, Los Angeles

Science Adviser: Terrence E. Young Jr., M.Ed., M.L.S.,
Jefferson (Louisiana) Public School System

First published in the United States in 2006 by
Compass Point Books
3109 West 50th St., #115
Minneapolis, MN 55410

ANIMAL KINGDOM CLASSIFICATION–WORMS
was produced by

David West Children's Books
7 Princeton Court
55 Felsham Road
London SW15 1AZ

Designer: David West
Editors: Gail Bushnell, Anthony Wacholtz, Kate Newport
Page Production: James Mackey

Visit Compass Point Books on the Internet at
www.compasspointbooks.com
or e-mail your request to
custserv@compasspointbooks.com

Library of Congress Cataloging-in-Publication Data
Parker, Steve.
  Nematodes, leeches & other worms / by Steve Parker.
    p. cm.—(Animal kingdom classification)
  Includes bibliographical references.
  ISBN 0-7565-1615-3 (hardcover)
  1. Worms—Juvenile literature. 2. Nematoda—Juvenile literature. 3. Leeches—Juvenile literature. I. Title: Nematodes, leeches, and other worms. II. Title. III. Series.
  QL386.6.P37 2006
  592'.3—dc22   2005029181

PHOTO CREDITS :
Abbreviations: t-top, m-middle, b-bottom, r-right, l-left, c-center.

Title page, Dr. James P. McVey, NOAA; 6/7, Melissa King, iStockphoto.com; 8t, 8b, Oxford Scientific Films; 9l, Melissa King, 9r, National Undersearch Research Program (NURP) Collection, 9b, Oxford Scientific Films; 11, Oxford Scientific Films; 12l, NOAA National Estuarine Research Reserve Collection, 12r, Oxford Scientific Films; 14-15, all Oxford Scientific Films; 16l,16r, Oxford Scientific Films; 17b, Oxford Scientific Films; 18-19, all Oxford Scientific Films; 20l, Grace Tan , 20t, 20r, Oxford Scientific Films; 21l, 21r, Oxford Scientific Films; 22t, Oxford Scientific Films; 23t, Oxford Scientific Films, 23b, NOAA National Estuarine Research Reserve Collection; 24t, Collection of Dr. James P. McVey, NOAA Sea Grant Program, 24b, James Guttuso; 25tl, C. Van Dover, 25tr, 25b, Oxford Scientific Films; 26r, Oxford Scientific Films; 26l, Oxford Scientific Films; 26tr. NOAA; 26b, Oxford Scientific Films; 28/29(all), Oxford Scientific Films; 30/31(all), Oxford Scientific Films; 32, Oxford Scientific Films; 32/33, Oxford Scientific Films; 32/33t, Dan Scmitt, istockphoto.com; 33, Oxford Scientific Films; 34/35(all), Oxford Scientific Films; 36/37, Oxford Scientific Films; 36, Professor Dr. V. Stoich.; 37, Oxford Scientific Films; 38, Oxford Scientific Films; 38/39, OAR/National Undersea Research Program (NURP); 39, Oxford Scientific Films; 40, Linda Kuhnz © 2003 MBARI; 40/41, Oxford Scientific Films; 41, Oxford Scientific Films; 42, Oxford Scientific Films; 42/43,Oxford Scientific Films; 43t, Oxford Scientific Films

With special thanks to the models: Felix Blom, Tucker Bryant, and Margaux Monfared.

Front cover: Tube worm
Opposite: Flatworm

ANIMAL KINGDOM CLASSIFICATION

NEMATODES, LEECHES & OTHER
WORMS

Steve Parker

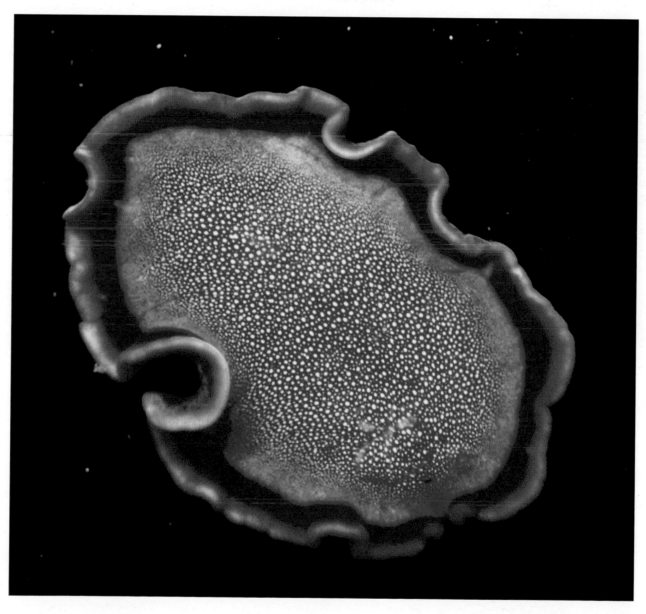

COMPASS POINT BOOKS MINNEAPOLIS, MINNESOTA

TABLE OF CONTENTS

INTRODUCTION	6	WORM REPRODUCTION	18
WORMS ALMOST EVERYWHERE	8	SUCKERS!	20
INSIDE A WORM	10	SEASHORE WORMS	22
WORMS WITH SEGMENTS	12	FANS, FEATHERS, AND TUBES	24
RECYCLING NATURE	14	WORM HEADS	26
HOW WORMS MOVE	16	ROUNDWORMS	28

HAIRS AND SPINES   30

FLATS AND TAPES   32

VERY LONG, VERY THIN   34

SECRET WORMS OF THE SEABED 36

PEANUTS AND HORSESHOES   38

BEARDS AND ARROWS   40

GREAT WORM MYSTERIES   42

ANIMAL CLASSIFICATION   44

ANIMAL PHYLA   45

GLOSSARY   46

FURTHER RESOURCES   47

INDEX   48

INTRODUCTION

Worms are usually long, thin, slimy, and squirmy. They make some people squirm, too. Yet the earthworms that tunnel under our gardens, back yards, parks, and fields, are just a few of the many thousands of species of worms. Some live in water, where we never see them, and some are not even the typical worm shape—they look like colored fans or flowers.

Worms are vital for the balance of nature. Many eat old, rotting, or decaying plants and animals, and so naturally recycle lots of nutrients. In turn they become food for many creatures, from crabs and fish to frogs, birds, moles, and shrews. Without worms, the natural world would soon grind to a halt.

NATURE'S GARDENERS

Earthworms are our friends. They eat their way through soil and leaves, making burrows that let in light, air, and water. In this way they enrich the soil and help plants grow.

Different kinds of worms live in almost all types of habitats, or surroundings, on Earth. They burrow in the mud of the deepest seabed, swim through the wide ocean, dig in sandy beaches, tunnel into wood, burrow in grasslands, and even survive in the thin soil of deserts and high mountains.

GROUPS OF WORMS

There are about a dozen main animal groups, or phyla, of wormlike creatures. They include flatworms in mountain streams, ribbon worms along seashores, arrowworms of the open sea, and peanut worms on the ocean floor. Worms live almost anywhere that is watery or damp—including the insides of other living things.

Types of worms called tapeworms, flukes, and roundworms live as parasites inside many animals, from fish and birds to shrews and whales. A parasite takes essential needs such as nutrients and shelter from its host creature, and in the process harms it. Almost every kind of animal can catch its own form of worm parasite, including our farm animals, our pets—and ourselves.

LUGWORM CASTS (COASTAL)

ROUNDWORMS (PARASITIC)

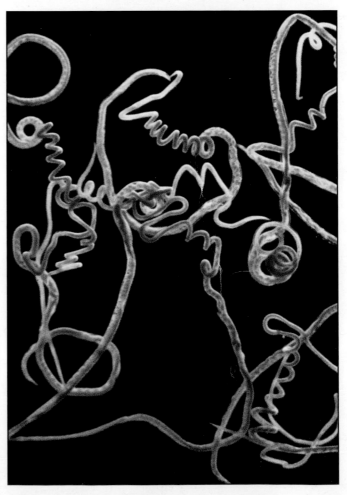

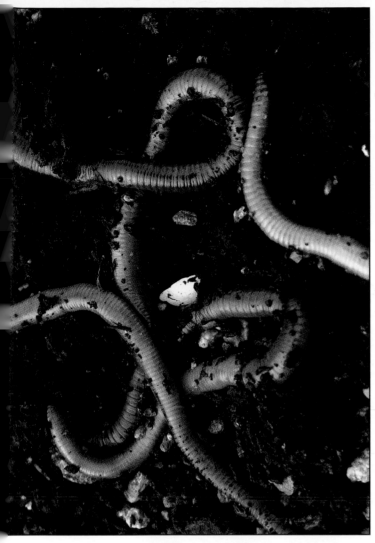

EARTHWORMS (TERRESTRIAL)

TUBE WORMS (MARINE)

AMAZING NUMBERS

In daily life most people do not come across worms, unless digging the garden or using them as bait for fishing. But worms exist in incredible numbers. A patch of rich soil the size of a single bed may contain over 1,000 earthworms, from tiny babies to full-grown adults. This soil may also contain more than 1 million nematodes or roundworms, most too small to see.

Worms are usually out of sight, in soil or under the water, and we do not get to see them in huge numbers.

INSIDE A WORM

An earthworm may look like a simple tube, which takes in soil at the front end, digests any nutritious pieces, and pushes out the leftovers at the rear end. But inside, it is much more complicated.

BODY SYSTEMS

A worm has blood, nerves, muscles, and guts, just like most other animals. Almost the whole way along its body is a fluid-filled space called the coelom, or body cavity. At the front, the main nerve has a ganglion, or enlarged lump, which is a simple brain. Most types of worms have these basic body parts. But only certain groups of worms have a segmented structure. This means that the body is made of a long row of many similar ringed sections called segments.

MUSCLE SYSTEM

There are two main layers of muscles, shown in the cross section diagram below. The ringlike circular ones shorten to make the body narrower and longer. The ribbon-shaped longitudinal muscles contract to make the body shorter and fatter. Together they allow the worm to wriggle and bend itself into almost any shape.

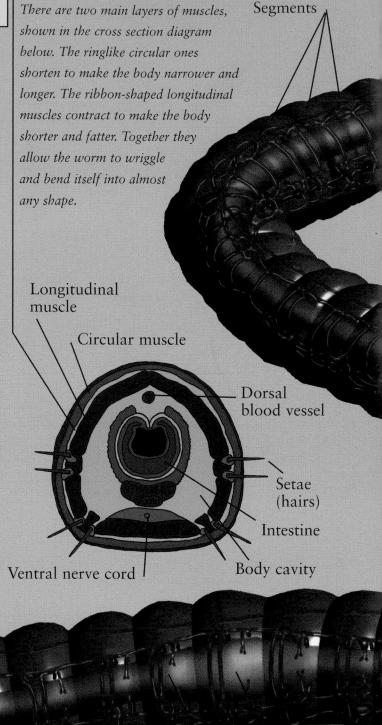

Segments

Longitudinal muscle

Circular muscle

Dorsal blood vessel

Setae (hairs)

Intestine

Ventral nerve cord

Body cavity

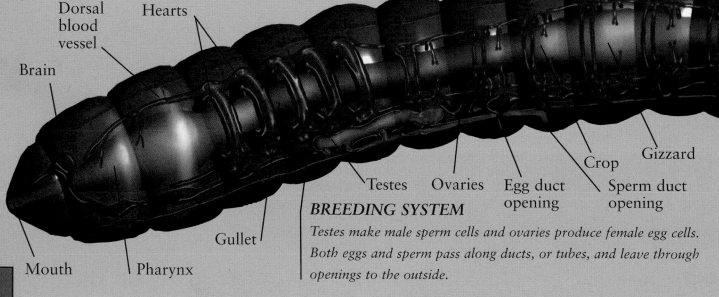

Dorsal blood vessel

Hearts

Brain

Gizzard

Crop

Testes   Ovaries   Egg duct opening   Sperm duct opening

Gullet

Mouth   Pharynx

BREEDING SYSTEM

Testes make male sperm cells and ovaries produce female egg cells. Both eggs and sperm pass along ducts, or tubes, and leave through openings to the outside.

Tail

Anus

NERVE SYSTEM

The ventral (lower) nerve cord along the base of the body carries signals to control body parts, especially muscles.

DIGESTIVE SYSTEM

The long gut tube that runs through the body has specialized regions. The pharynx takes in food, the crop stores it, the gizzard grinds it, and the long intestine digests it.

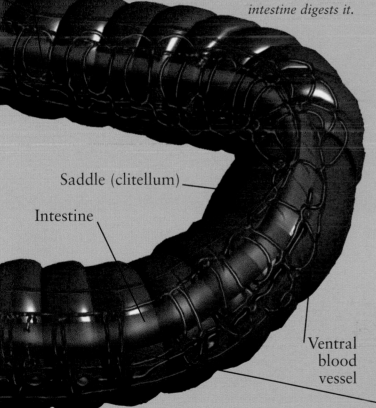

Saddle (clitellum)

Intestine

Ventral blood vessel

BLOOD SYSTEM

Blood flows along the dorsal (upper) blood vessel from the worm's tail to its head. Then it dips down through five pairs of "hearts" whose thick muscular walls provide the pumping power. As the blood then flows toward the tail in the ventral (lower) vessel, it seeps up through tiny vessels in the body to the main dorsal vessel again.

WORM SKIN

The skin, or outer layer, of a worm is called its cuticle. In worms that live in drier places it is usually thick and covered with mucus. Like our own skin, the cuticle of the earthworm replaces or renews itself nonstop, because its outer layers rub off when pushing past soil particles. However, the cuticle does not just provide protection for earthworms; it also works like our lungs, taking in oxygen, which all animals need to survive.

A layer of mucus, or slime, enables the worm to slip through soil more easily and also helps to stop it drying out.

One of the biggest groups of worms is the annelids, or segmented worms. It includes earthworms, seashore ragworms, lugworms, tube worms, fan worms, and even blood-sucking leeches.

WHAT ARE SEGMENTS?

There are at least 12,000 species, or kinds, of annelids. Their main feature is a body divided into a long row of ringed sections called segments. It is because of their appearance that annelids are also known as "ringed worms." Earthworm segments are obvious, and some have more than 200 of them. But other annelids have a smoother body outline where the segmented structure is less clear on the outside.

RING AFTER RING

The segments are easy to see on this tiny detritus worm against the rotting material in a compost heap. The prostomium, or front section, is not a true segment—it has a different structure.

RED AS BLOOD

Named after their bright red color, bloodworms are annelids that usually live in slow-flowing, swampy, or stagnant water. Like earthworms, each segment has tiny hairs called setae.

WHAT ARE SEGMENTS?

Each segment has a similar pattern of smaller parts inside, including blood vessels, nerves, and muscles. However, some segments have a slightly different structure, such as those containing the animal's breeding or waste-disposing parts. The worm's main blood vessels, nerve, and gut usually run along inside the whole chain of segments.

Throughout millions of years of prehistory, worms with their soft bodies left few hard remains as fossils in the rocks. But some rare examples have been preserved, and they show that wormlike creatures were among the first true animals in the seas more than 500 million years ago. Ottoia was a priapulid worm about 5 inches (13 cm) long, with a spiny head ①, buried body, and spiky tail ②. Burgessochaeta ③ was a ragwormlike annelid. Hallucigenia ④ was an extraordinary creature with a worm-shaped body, tall spikes on its back, and pairs of legs like stilts. Pikaia ⑤ was a very early form of a creature, called the lancelet, that resembled a fish.

RECYCLING NATURE

Worms are vital in most habitats because they recycle nutrients, minerals, and other substances in the soil. This allows plants to grow, providing food for many animals.

FOOD CHAINS AND WEBS

Food chains begin with green plants growing in the soil. Herbivorous animals eat shoots, leaves, fruits, and other plant parts. Carnivorous creatures prey on herbivores and each other. In this way food chains build up and connect with each other to form food webs.

BRANDLING WORM

Up to 5 inches (13 cm) long and covered with yellow rings, this worm lives in compost heaps.

VITAL LINKS

Worms, especially earthworms, play important roles in these ecosystems. One role is to keep the soil rich and healthy so plants can grow, and another is to recycle the soil's nutrients.

CHEWY FOOD

Earthworms pull old leaves and other plant parts into their burrows to eat, to block the entrance, and to keep in moisture. This moves rotting material from the surface into the soil.

HEALTHY SOIL

Soil and earth that are squeezed and squashed contain little air and only trapped, stagnant water. Plant roots prefer more open, spongy soil that allows in air and trickling water. Earthworms open up the soil with their burrows and tunnels. The tunnels also allow in light for microscopic plants that grow near the surface. These tiny plants are food for very small animals and form tiny food chains that in turn make the soil rich in nutrients.

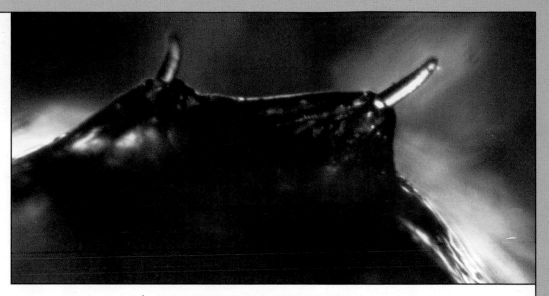

EARTHWORM BRISTLES

A close-up of an earthworm's body shows a pair of tiny hairs, called setae. There are four pairs on each segment. As the worm tunnels, it presses the setae on one part of its body into the sides of the tunnel for anchorage, while another part of the body slides along.

ROUND AGAIN

All living things eventually die. Then worms, fungi, and other decomposers cause their bodies to rot. This releases the nutrients and minerals stored in the dead bodies into the soil. The nutrients are then carried up into plant roots and eventually to the plant where they are needed for growth.

Earthworms are an essential part of this process. They eat all kinds of soil particles and expel what they don't need in a more broken-down form, ideal for plant growth.

GIANT WORMS

In a few parts of the world, earthworms are giants. These huge species live in southern Africa and South Australia. They are very similar to ordinary earthworms, but much bigger. As they slide through their slime-lined tunnels, they make gurgling noises that can be heard hundreds of feet away.

Giant earthworms grow to more than 6 feet (1.8 m) long, with a body as thick as an adult man's thumb.

HOW WORMS MOVE

BURROWING

An earthworm shortens longitudinal, or lengthways, muscles in its rear half to make them wide and fat, and presses them against the tunnel wall. Then it contracts circular muscles at the front, which becomes long and thin, and thrusts through the soil.

Worms may seem to wriggle and writhe but do little else. Yet the two simple layers of muscles in an earthworm's body enable it to perform many kinds of actions and movements. Other kinds of worms in different habitats move in very unusual ways.

WATER-FILLED BALLOON

A soft, floppy earthworm can quickly become stiff and hard. Its body is like a fluid-filled tube. When both layers of muscles around this tube shorten or contract, they press on the fluid. It's like squeezing a sausage-shaped, water-filled balloon—the worm has a "skeleton" made of pressurized fluid. This is called a hydrostatic skeleton.

The worm can make different regions of its muscles contract at different times. If it shortens the ribbonlike longitudinal muscles on the left side near the front, its head end bends to the left. These simple actions build up into complicated ones—a worm can even tie itself in a knot!

S-SHAPED SWIMMER

The leech, an annelid, shortens the longitudinal muscles along the top of its body to bend its head up. Then it contracts the muscles beneath to arch down. By doing this many times, the leech swims by making up-and-down undulations, like S-shaped "waves" moving along its body.

OPEN FANS

Fan worms are annelids, like earthworms and leeches. The delicate feathery "fan" opens to collect tiny particles of floating food. If danger comes near, muscles in the worm's body contract to whisk the "fan" down into the protective tube.

THE ROWING RAGWORM

The seashore ragworm has a series of flaps along its body, one on each side of each segment. The flaps are called parapodia and they carry the tiny setae hairs, as well as small "tentacles" that sense touch and water currents. Muscles inside the parapodia tilt them as the ragworm bends its body to wriggle along. This helps to give the worm a "rowing" motion like paddling a boat.

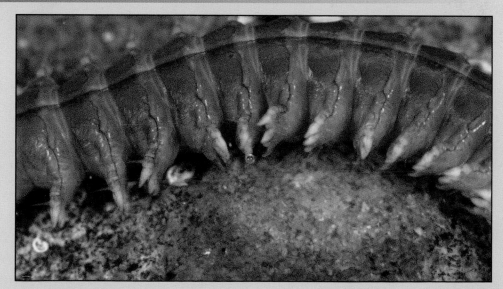

The flaplike parapodia along a ragworm's sides wave like tiny paddles to help the worm swim or "row" through sand and mud.

WORM REPRODUCTION

Worms breed, or reproduce, in many different ways. Some worms are like many other animals; a female and male come together and mate, and then the female lays eggs. But some worms are both female and male.

GETTING TOGETHER

Earthworms usually mate on damp nights, when their moist bodies are at less risk of drying out, and they cannot be seen by predators like birds.

MATING

An animal that has both female and male breeding parts in the same body is called a hermaphrodite. Many kinds of annelid worms, including earthworms and leeches, are hermaphrodites. However, each one still has to get together and mate with another of its kind. When this happens, each worm passes male sperm to the other, where they join with female eggs. Then each worm lays its eggs, which hatch into tiny baby worms.

COCOONS

Earthworms and many other annelids lay their eggs in protective containers called cocoons. These are made of slimy substances produced by the worm itself. In earthworms, the cocoon is made by larger segments toward the head end, called the clitellum or saddle.

Earthworms come to the surface to mate. The two worms lie partly overlapping, head-to-tail, and exchange sperm. On each worm, the clitellum makes a mucus cocoon shaped like a collar. The worm wriggles out of this, leaving its 20 or so eggs inside. The cocoon hardens while the eggs inside develop and hatch.

BROKEN WORMS

Certain kinds of worms, mainly annelid worms in the sea, can increase their numbers simply by breaking into pieces. Their bodies are designed to come apart at certain places. Some of the resulting fragments regenerate, or grow, whole new bodies. This process is rare in earthworms, where usually only a fairly complete head end can regenerate a new tail.

LEAVING THE COCOON

After the cocoon has slipped off the adult worm, the eggs inside grow and develop. They have a store of food in the form of yolk, plus a nutritious fluid called albumen around them. After a few weeks, the baby worms squirm out of the cocoon to begin their burrowing lives.

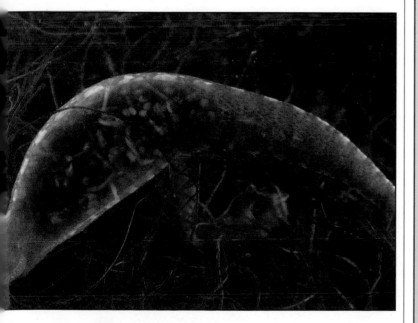

PIGGYBACK RIDE

Some worms, including various leeches, brood their eggs. This means that they stay near the cocoon or carry it with them. Newly hatched babies of the theromyzon leech attach to the underside of their parent, who carries them to their first meal of blood.

THE CLITELLUM (SADDLE)

The clitellum is an enlarged series of segments that make the breeding cocoon and the nutritious fluid inside it. The position of the clitellum, in terms of the numbers of its segments, is important when identifying very similar species of earthworms.

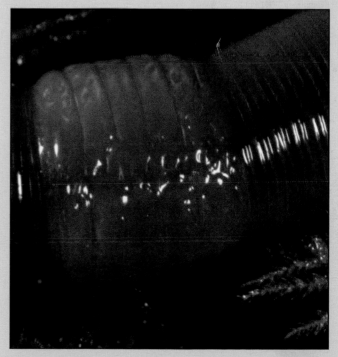

The segments of the clitellum are usually larger and paler than the other body parts.

SUCKERS!

Blood is a complete food, and various animals feed on nothing else, from vampire bats to fleas—and leeches. There are about 600 kinds of leeches living in most parts of the world, mainly in freshwater.

WORM "VAMPIRES"

Leeches form the subgroup called Hirudinea within the main annelid group. Only a few kinds feed solely on blood. Others are predators, hunting down tiny creatures such as baby worms, snails, and fish in ponds, rivers, lakes, ditches, and canals. A few kinds can live in damp forests where they glide among the wet leaves and shelter under boulders and logs. The biggest leeches can reach up to 8 inches (20 cm) long when stretched out.

A HUGE MEAL
The leech's body is like a stretchy balloon bag that expands to hold its liquid food. Some leeches suck up five times their own weight in blood. This can contain enough nourishment to last them a year.

FISH SUCKERS
Sucking leeches infest all kinds of water animals, especially fish, such as the stickleback. The leech can suck blood or body fluids through the thin covering of the fish's gills or through its skin between the body scales.

WATER DANGER
As a blood-sucking leech feeds, it releases an anesthetic substance into the wound, so its live host hardly feels the blood loss.

MEDICINAL LEECH

For centuries, people believed that various diseases were caused by too much or "impure" blood in the body. Their answer was to allow leeches to suck out some, and then encourage the bleeding to continue after the leech had been removed in a process called bloodletting. The main type of leech that was used for this has become known as the medicinal leech or *Hirudo medicinalis*.

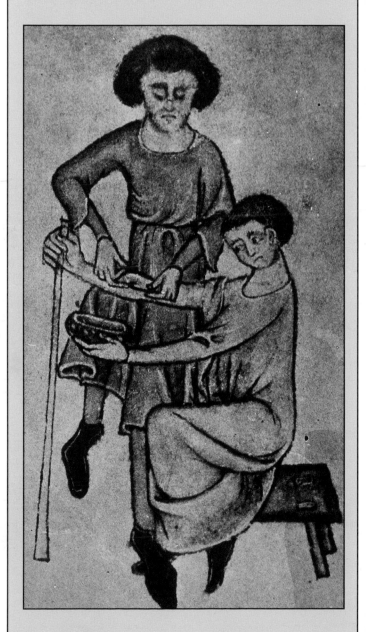

A medicinal leech produces an anticoagulant substance that stops blood clotting.

DEVELOPING BABIES

Young leeches develop inside a protective cocoon made by the parent. When hatched, these young medicinal leeches will feed on the blood of small fish and amphibians, such as frogs. As they grow, they move to mammals like horses and cattle.

LEECH DESIGN

Most leeches have a leaf-shaped body with 33 segments. There is a sucker under the narrower head and another under the rear end. The leech attaches its rear sucker, stretches its body forward, attaches the head end, then draws up the tail behind, in a type of movement called "looping."

Some leeches have a proboscis—a tubelike mouth armed with hard "teeth," which can poke out and scrape the skin of the host to release blood. Others have a powerful mouth that works like a sucker to gulp in tiny prey.

SEASHORE WORMS

All around the world, the sea's shores and shallows are wriggling and crawling with worms. Many belong to the annelid subgroup called the polychaetes, or bristleworms, such as lugworms and ragworms.

BEACH LIFE

Lugworms may not be seen often. But their droppings are familiar as the squiggly worm casts dotted in the thousands along beaches at low tide, similar to earthworm casts found on garden lawns.

Each lugworm lives in the lower part of a U-shaped burrow. As it eats sand, a shallow bowllike pit forms on the surface at one end of the U, above the worm's head. After the worm digests the nutrients, the sand leaves the worm's rear end and is pushed up to the surface, forming the cast.

LIVING UNDERGROUND
The lugworm makes a sticky mucus lining for its burrow so the sand or mud does not collapse. The thicker part (above) is its front end, and the whole body can grow to 8 inches (20 cm) long.

TWISTED TANGLE
A lugworm's cast forms outside its burrow above its tail. About 4-8 inches (10-20 cm) away under the sand is the head end of the lugworm.

FIERCE HUNTER

The ragworm or sandworm is a busy predator on beaches and in rock pools. It can wriggle or "row" with the flaps along its body to move through sand and mud. It has no home burrow, but wanders in search of live prey or dead bodies to scavenge. To capture food, it pokes out its tubelike proboscis, which is tipped with stabbing "jaws." Large ragworms, like the king ragworm, grow to more than 16 inches (40 cm) long and have a powerful bite that easily draws blood through human skin.

KING OF THE ROCK POOL

Big ragworms prey on all kinds of smaller creatures, including shrimps, prawns, sea snails, baby fish, and other worms.

BIRD FOOD

Sandy and muddy beaches teem with worms and other life, which we cannot usually see because they are below the surface. However, wading birds recognize surface signs of creatures below and use their sensitive beak tip to probe and detect movement. Smaller waders with short beaks, like dunlin and dowitchers, reach just below the surface with fast jabs. Larger waders, like the curlew, probe more slowly and as far as 12 inches (30 cm) down.

At low tide, flocks of waders like dowitchers poke into the mud for worms and similar food.

FANS, FEATHERS, AND TUBES

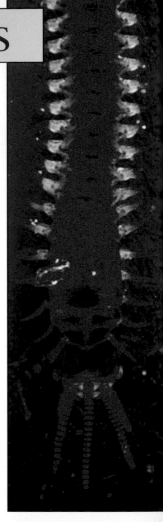

S ome of the most beautiful creatures of the sea look like multicolored fans, feather dusters, and delicate flowers, yet they are worms. The fan worms are specialized to feed on tiny particles floating in the water.

PEACOCK WORMS
The tubelike home of a fan worm can stick up above the sand's surface by 4 inches (10 cm) with another 8 inches (20 cm) buried below.

BREATHE AND FEED
The "fan" of a fan worm is a series of long, thin tentacles forming an almost circular "crown" at the head end. They work both as gills, to take in oxygen from the water, and as a feeding device. They are covered with a thin layer of sticky mucus that traps all kinds of tiny bits and pieces floating in the water.

PARCHMENT WORM
A parchment worm lives in a 16 inch (40 cm) tube that feels leathery, like old parchment.

SORTED OUT
Micro-hairs called cilia, fringing the tentacles, wave steadily like tiny oars to make the tiny particles flow down to the head where they are sorted. Nutritious ones, including the tiny eggs and young of sea creatures, enter the mouth. Others are passed farther along the worm's body to build the tube in which it lives. The rest are thrown away.

CLEAR-WATER COLOR
Most fan worms, like the scarlet fan worm, live in warm, clear waters. Too much floating sediment, like sand or mud particles, clogs up their tentacles.

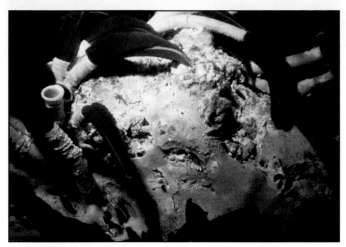

BOTTOM OF THE SEA

Deep-sea tube worms as thick as a human arm and 6 feet (1.8 m) long live around hydrothermal vents. These are places where hot water laden with minerals and chemicals spurts up through cracks in the seabed from deep in the earth.

SETTING UP HOUSE

Most tube worms construct hard tubular shelters from particles of minerals in the water around. As the worms die and more set up home on top, the colony grows in the manner of a coral reef.

TUBE WORMS

Like fan worms, tube worms are in the polychaete subgroup of annelids and live in the sea. Each makes a hard tube of rocky minerals, from which it extends its frilly head tentacles to feed on the "soup" of floating particles called plankton.

Keelworms are small tube worms that make squiggly, whitish tubes from chalk minerals. A sharp edge or keel runs along the tube. Tube worms live attached to any hard surfaces like a boulder, the shell of a whelk or mussel, or even a crab or lobster.

SEA MOUSE

The sea mouse may look like a furry mammal. But it is a type of polychaete scale worm that burrows just beneath the surface of sand, below the low-tide mark. It has silky grey "fur" on its back and thicker brown bristles and glistening gold-green hairs along its lower edges. These are all types of hairs called chaetae.

The sea mouse grows to about 4 inches (10 cm) long.

WORM HEADS

Worms have a huge variety of head ends, from the fragile tentacles of a fan worm to the tough-nosed burrowing front end of the earthworm. The head end also holds the sensors for touch, chemicals, and light in the form of simple "eyes."

FRONT END

The basic parts of an annelid worm's head include two pairs of light sensors or "eyes," three long feelers or antennae, two sensitive fingerlike palps, tiny chemical- and motion-detecting hairs known as cirri, and perhaps a proboscis or "snout." Some snouts can be withdrawn, like pushing the finger of an empty glove inside-out.

Most worms have some of their head parts missing, but others are large and well-developed. It depends on which are most useful in their particular habitat. The "eyes" cannot form images but only sense patches of light and dark.

EUNICE WORM
One of the largest predatory worms at over 6 feet (1.8 m) long, the eunice worm has two eyes, five antennae, and a very sharp bite.

FINE FANS
The fan worm's "crown" of tentacles is very sensitive to ripples, currents, and light. If an object looms near and casts a shadow, the worm can contract down into its tube in less than a second.

GIANT BEACHWORM

The Australian giant beachworm can grow to be 8 feet (2.5 m) long. It feeds on small shellfish, like cockles, as well as dead creatures.

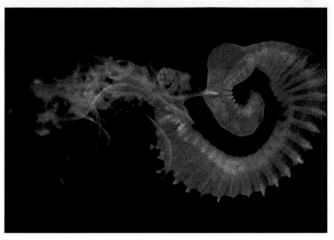

SPAGHETTI WORM

The feeding tentacles grow to 3 feet (.9 m) long. The worm's main body is usually protected in a buried tube and can grow to 1 foot (30 cm) long.

CLEANING THE REEF

Many worms are detritivores, eating detritus—the mix of small bits and pieces from dead animals and plants, as found in soil or on the seabed. Spaghetti worms each live in a tube buried in sand or mud, or in a rocky crack. The worm makes its own "glue" and sticks together bits of sand and shell fragments to build the tube.

The head end has a mass of long feeding tentacles. These wriggle and feel the seabed for small bits of food. As in the fan worm, micro-hairs called cilia beat to move edible particles along each tentacle to the mouth. In this way spaghetti worms clean the seabed and recycle nutrients.

SCALE WORMS

Scale worms are polychaete worms with overlapping hard plates like fish scales along their back. Most scaleworms are small, less than an inch (2.5 cm) long, and live a sheltered life under seaweeds and stones. Some kinds can make their scales glow with "living light," a process called bioluminescence.

Scale worms are common on the lower shore.

ROUNDWORMS

It is difficult to find a habitat that lacks roundworms or nematodes. They are mostly small, tough, and incredibly numerous—and some kinds infest millions of people.

SIMPLE PLAN

Roundworms do not have segments, like annelid worms. Their body plan is a simple tube with a mouth at one end, gut and muscle strands and several nerve cords along the middle, and the exit hole or anus near the rear end. There are few sensory parts like antennae or hairs.

MOST WIDESPREAD ANIMALS

There are more than 15,000 different species of roundworms, with new ones discovered regularly. They live virtually everywhere, from thin soil on mountains to the ooze of deep-sea trenches. The body covering or cuticle is thick and tough, allowing some nematodes to survive in hot springs and others in vinegar as eelworms. A handful of rich soil teems with many hundreds of microscopic roundworms.

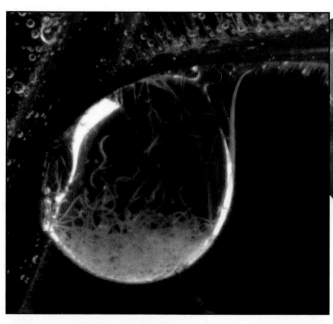

TRICHOSTRONGYLUS

This tiny hairlike roundworm, only ⅕ of an inch (5 mm) long, lives in the stomach of cattle, sheep, and horses. Too many can kill their host.

PORK ROUNDWORM

The pig roundworm Ascaris affects more than 1 billion people around the world. Its eggs usually get into the body when people eat undercooked pork. It can grow to 16 inches (40 cm) long and lives inside the intestine.

HUNTERS

Some roundworms are free-roaming hunters. They search out tinier creatures as prey, writhing through water or soil with a characteristic C or S shape movement.

PARASITES

Hundreds of types of roundworms live as parasites inside plants or other creatures. In the process they cause many kinds of serious diseases, like eelworms on plant roots. Roundworms that infest people include hookworms and threadworms, or pinworms, in the intestine, and filarial worms. The tropical filarial worm Wucheria is spread by mosquitoes. It blocks fluid tubes in the human body known as lymph channels, especially in the legs. This causes the massive wrinkled swellings known as elephantiasis.

THREADWORMS

Threadworms, Enterobius, are small pale roundworms that live in the human intestine. At night the females emerge through the intestine's end, the anus, to lay eggs. The female worm also makes an irritating fluid, which causes the person to scratch and pick up the eggs under their fingernails. If the person puts their fingers in their mouth, they swallow the eggs, starting another infestation.

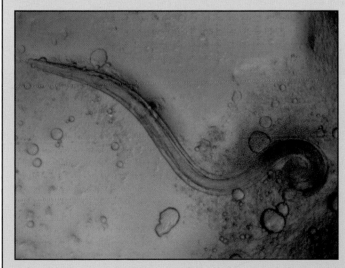

Threadworms are about ²/₅ of an inch (1 cm) long.

NIPPOSTRONGYLUS

This roundworm thrives in rat intestines. Like many roundworms, it is a parasite only when adult, and it lives as a larva in the soil.

HAIRS AND SPINES

Horsehair worms live around ponds, ditches, and the drinking troughs of farm animals like horses. A bunch of them look just like a tangle of horse's hair come to life, which could explain their name.

YOUNG PARASITES

Horsehair worms make up their own major animal group, the phylum Nematomorpha. This means "nematode-shaped" because from the outside, horsehair worms look like roundworms.

There are fewer than 100 species of horsehair worms, and most live in fresh water as adults. The females lay eggs that hatch into young larvae and get into insects such as grasshoppers and cockroaches. The larvae live there as parasites, sometimes for several months, before leaving to become adults.

TWO HOSTS FOR ONE WORM

Most spiny-headed worms have two hosts. When they are young, as larvae, they infest insects, spiders, and crustaceans such as crabs and shrimps. Then they get into a bigger, second host such as a fish or bird—often when this eats the first host. The female and male worms mate inside the second host. The female lays eggs that pass out with the host's droppings, a first-stage host eats the eggs, and the cycle repeats.

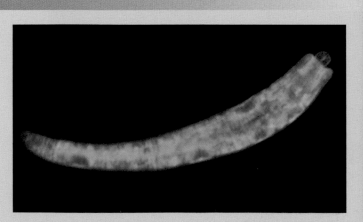

Spiny-headed worms have a spiky proboscis.

TANGLED TOGETHER

Some kinds of horsehair worms reach about 3 feet (.9 m) in length. They shed or molt their thick cuticle or "skin" several times as they grow.

NOT HUNGRY

Many horsehair worms do all their feeding as larvae. After they become adults, they find others of their kind, mate, and then die.

SPINY-HEADS

Another main group of worms is the phylum Acanthocephala, a name which means "spiny-head." A spiny-headed worm has a fingerlike proboscis at its front end, which can be drawn into its head, or poked out to reveal its tip, which is armed with sharp curving hooks or spines. There are about 750 different species of spiny-headed worms. Most are less than an inch long but some grow to more than 3 feet (.9 m).

Spiny-headed worms do not have a mouth. They live as parasites inside the guts of various animals, surrounded by nutrients that the animal is digesting from its food. So the worm simply soaks up nutrients through its body covering. Its hook-covered proboscis is used to anchor it into the wall of the gut so it is not swept away by food passing through.

31

FLATS AND TAPES

The simplest worms are known as platyhelminths. There are about 13,000 species, which include the leaf-shaped flatworms of tropical forest floors, ponds, streams, and the sea, and two large groups of parasites, the flukes and the ribbonlike tapeworms.

FLAT BODIES

The body plan of platyhelminths is very simple. Some kinds have a mouth, but the gut is like a pouch inside the body, with no exit or exit hole—leftovers come back out of the mouth. There is also no heart or blood system as nutrients and other substances simply seep through the body. There is a lump of nerves at the head end for the "brain," as in the earthworm, but no proper segments.

MATING FLUKES

Most platyhelminths are both male and female in one body. Blood flukes have separate sexes.

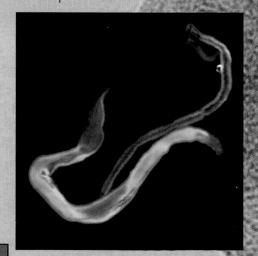

HOOKED HEAD

The tapeworm's tiny head end is smaller than this "o" and hooks into the gut lining of its host.

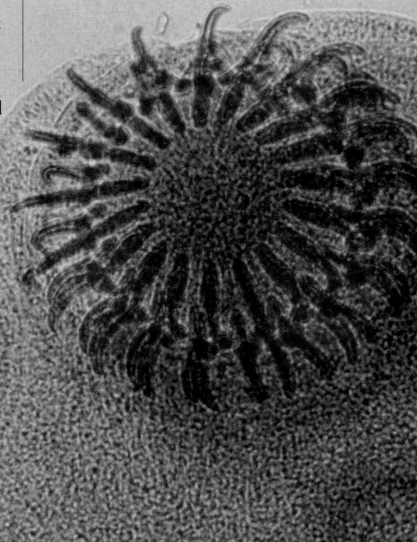

OUTSIDE AND INSIDE

A second platyhelminth group is the trematodes. Some of these live as external parasites on the skin of various creatures, especially fish, where they cling to the gills and suck blood. Others are the flukes or digeans, which live inside the bodies of many creatures, from fish to snakes, birds, whales, and humans. The $1/2$ of an inch (1.3 cm) blood fluke *Schistosoma* and the leaflike $1 \, 1/3$ inches (3.4 cm) liver fluke *Fasciola* infest millions of people in tropical regions.

WANDERING PREDATORS

One group of platyhelminths is the turbellarians. They are commonly known as flatworms or planarians and are found in all kinds of water. Many are difficult to spot, partly because they are colored or camouflaged to match their surroundings, and partly because they hide under stones.

TWO HOSTS

The third main platyhelminth group is the cestodes or tapeworms. All are internal parasites. Different fish, frogs, reptiles, birds, and mammals all have their own kinds of tapeworms, which often spend the early part of their life in another host. For example, the cat tapeworm, in its early stages, lives in mice. Tapeworms lie in the host's gut, soaking up nourishment. What look like their body segments are really separate "bags" of sex parts and eggs, called proglottids.

LEFT AND RIGHT

Flatworms are the simplest animals with a left and right side, in addition to an upper and lower surface, and a head and tail end. Simpler animals like jellyfish have a circular body plan. The flatworm's body is so thin that no part is far from the skin. A flatworm does not need special breathing parts like lungs or gills. Vital oxygen easily passes from the water, through the skin to all its inner parts.

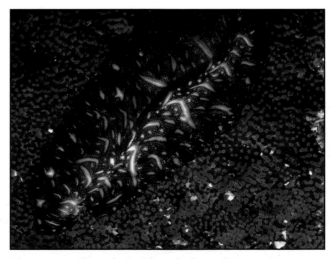

Flatworms "breathe" through their skin.

VERY LONG, VERY THIN

The longest animal on Earth is not a snake or a whale—it is a worm. Bootlace worms grow to an astonishing 120 feet (36.6 m) or more in length. However, their bodies are very slim and flattened, as suggested by another of their common names, ribbon worms.

SEASHORE HAZARDS

Ribbon worms make up the phylum Nemertea, with about 1,200 species. They live mainly along the seashore or in shallow waters. Some kinds burrow in sand and mud, while others coil under boulders or in rock crevices. A few are found in freshwater or in damp places on land.

Some ribbon worms, including the common bootlace worm, are drab dark brown or black. However, others have bright stripes, either all along the body or around it in a ringed pattern.

SINGLE CHOCOLATE STRIPE
The one-striped ribbon worm lives in the Pacific region and grows to about 3 feet (.9 m) in length.

MEATY MEALS

All ribbon worms are carnivores, or flesh-eaters. Some catch their own prey, mostly tiny water creatures or the young of worms, shellfish, and similar animals. Others scavenge on the dead bodies of larger creatures like fish.

LONGEST OF ALL?

Why ribbon worms grow to such incredible lengths is not clear. Often they are pecked by birds, snipped by crabs, or crushed by wave-hit boulders. Provided the head end is intact, it can grow a new, shorter tail end. Very long specimens are difficult to untangle and measure, but there are claims for lengths of over 150 feet (45.7 m).

USEFUL WEAPON

Another name for the ribbon worm is proboscis worm. This is because of their proboscis—a long fingerlike "snout" just in front of the mouth. It can be drawn into a pocket or pouch on the front of the head end or pumped up with body fluids and poked out to wave around.

In some ribbon worms the proboscis has sharp toothlike stylets at the end, to jab into and grab prey. In others it can be looped around a victim, in the way an elephant picks up a branch with its trunk. The proboscis then passes the meal into the mouth. The ribbon worm's body lacks segments, but it does have a simple brain, a blood system, and a gut that runs straight-through from mouth to exit hole.

LONG PROBOSCIS

This ribbon worm has everted, or poked out, its long proboscis. At the head end there are usually very simple eyes, arranged in pairs. Some ribbon worms have over 100 pairs!

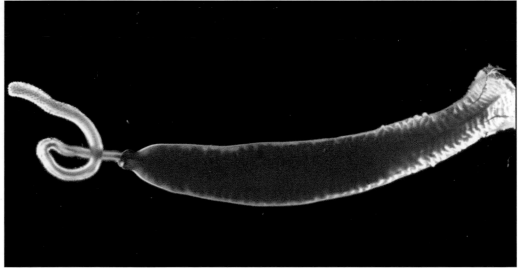

Ribbon worms are longer than nine adult elephants standing in a line!

SECRET WORMS OF THE SEABED

Some of the strangest worms live in the mud and sand of the seabed and are little known—even to scientists. They include the priapulid worms and the echiurans, usually called spoonworms.

ONLY A FEW

The priapulids make up one of the smallest of all phyla with only about 10 species. A priapulid worm has a large snout or proboscis that can be poked out and may have teeth to grab prey. The proboscis can be drawn into a headlike part, the introvert, which is also spiny or bristly.

GREEN SPOONWORM
The bright color warns predators that the skin is poisonous. The Y-shaped snout can reach up to 1 ½ feet (0.5 m).

TRUNK AND TAIL

A priapulid's main body or trunk is sausage shaped, with a gut running from the mouth to the exit hole at the end. The trunk usually has knobbly warts or pimples and may also show ringed marks, but these are not true segments. There is also a very long, narrow, bendy tail. This can help the worm to wriggle along, but in some kinds of priapulids, it has small hooks to anchor the priapulid in its burrow. The longest priapulid worms grow to about 10 in (25 cm) long, including the tail.

PRIAPULID WORM
The young form, or larva, of a priapulid worm is very slim and over 3 feet (.9 m) long. This adult has its proboscis to the left.

SHALLOW WATERS

Like priapulid worms, most spoonworms live in sand and mud near the shore or in shallow water. However, a few kinds are found at great depths of many thousands of feet. Spoonworms make up the phylum Echiura, with around 150 species.

LONG "TONGUE"

Also like a priapulid, a spoonworm has a proboscis, but this can be extended to several times the length of its body. It may also have a forked or branched tip. The proboscis is covered with sticky mucus and wriggles across the seabed "licking" up tiny bits of food.

MALES AND FEMALES

Priapulid worms are either male or female. The female lays eggs that hatch into larvae. These may drift in the ocean for up to two years before changing into the bottom-dwelling adults. In some spoonworms the males are tiny and live like parasites, sometimes even living inside the bodies of the females.

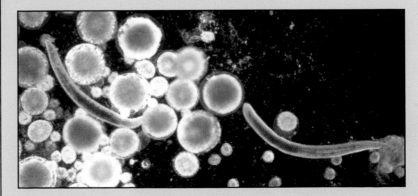

Tiny male spoonworms, smaller than the female's eggs

37

PEANUTS AND HORSESHOES

Peanut worms are well named. Many have light brown bodies shaped like peanuts, but others are longer, and look like plump sausages. These worms live on the seafloor, from shallow waters to enormous depths.

PEANUT WORM

Most peanut worms are 4 inches (10 cm) long, but some reach more than 1 ½ feet (0.5 m). The brown skin feels rough, like leathery sandpaper.

EXTENDING MOUTH

Peanut worms form the phylum Sipuncula, with about 350 species. Like spoonworms, a peanut worm has a very long, flexible, fingerlike head part which can be extended to up to 10 times the length of its body. This is called an introvert since it has the mouth at the tip, unlike the proboscis of a spoonworm.

LOOKING FOR LUNCH

When a peanut worm feeds, it extends and waves its introvert so that the mouth at the tip wanders across the seabed. Small frilly tentacles around the mouth gather tiny food particles with a sticky mucus. If the worm is touched, the long introvert instantly pulls back.

Some peanut worms wriggle into soft sand or mud to protect themselves in a temporary burrow. Others take over the empty shell of shellfish, such as a whelk, and hide inside. A few kinds can bore holes in rocks or coral.

HORSESHOE WORMS

These worms live in strong tubes buried in mud and sand and grow to 8 inches (20 cm) long.

U-SHAPED CROWN

Horseshoe worms, not to be confused with horsehair worms, are another very small worm phylum, named Phorona, or Phoronida, with only about 20 species. They are named after the shape of their "crown" of feeding tentacles, or lophophore. This forms a U or horseshoe when seen from above. The tentacles—which may number more than 10,000—are coated with a sticky mucus. They wave in the water to catch tiny pieces of food, which are passed to the mouth in their center.

BUDDING WORMS

Several kinds of worms, including horseshoe worms, can breed by "budding." A small new worm grows on the body of an adult, like a bud on a flower stem. Gradually the "bud" enlarges, then breaks away as a separate individual worm. In good conditions a few horseshoe worms can produce hundreds more by budding. They live together as a close group with their tentacles nearly touching.

Horseshoe worms form close-knit colonies.

BEARDS AND ARROWS

The great oceans still hold many surprises. The habits and functions of beard worms are still being uncovered. The arrowworm is a unique small, and transparent ocean dweller.

BEARD AT THE FRONT

Beard worms make up the phylum Pogonophora, with about 160 different species. They are among the slimmest of all worms for their length. Some are more than 3 feet (.9 m) long, but just $1/2$ of an inch wide and shaped more like a piece of wire than a worm.

Beard worms are named after the shaggy mass or "beard" of tentacles at the head end. The long and relatively stiff body is protected in a tough self-built tube buried in seabed sand or mud.

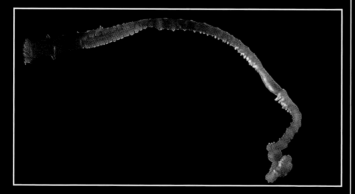

BEARD WORM
The beard worm has a very long body called the trunk. It bears little pimples or papillae to help movement within the tube, and the stubby enlarged ridged "tail," the opisthosoma, is thought to help the worm to burrow.

NO MOUTH

Beard worms are unusual among worms because they have no mouth or gut. They simply soak up nutritious substances dissolved in the water around them. The beard of tentacles might help with this. In the female, the tentacles also "grab" packets of sperm from the male, to join with the eggs, inside the female's tube. The young or larvae grow here, too, before leaving to find their own patch of muddy seabed.

DARTING "FLIGHT"

About 90 species of arrowworms form the phylum Chaetognatha. All live in the ocean, and almost all are found near the surface or in mid water, with just one species known to live on the seabed.

Arrowworms are small, slim, and transparent. There are two pairs of fishlike "fins" along the body and a kind of "tail fin." The similarity of the tail to an arrow's flight, and the arrowworm's very rapid darting movements, have given the group its name.

Arrowworms sometimes occur in vast swarms numbering tens of thousands. Due to their active lifestyle, each one needs plenty of nourishment and can eat its own weight in food in just four days. This means the huge swarms can have a devastating effect on the balance of ocean life. For example, if they eat large numbers of baby fish at breeding time, there will be a lack of older fish to feed hunters like barracudas and sharks.

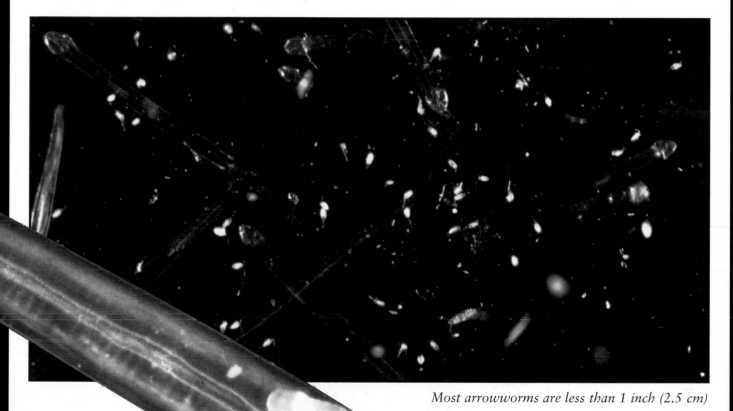

Most arrowworms are less than 1 inch (2.5 cm) long but can be 5 inches (13 cm) long.

SHARP TEETH

Arrowworms are very active hunters. They dart after all kinds of smaller creatures, including the young forms or larvae of shrimps, crabs, shellfish, and worms, which make up the plankton. Around the head end are many curved sharp "teeth" which grab the prey and jab it into the mouth. Most arrowworms have two small, simple eyes to detect light levels. Their bodies are covered with tiny tufts of hairs that sense ripples in the water.

41

GREAT WORM MYSTERIES

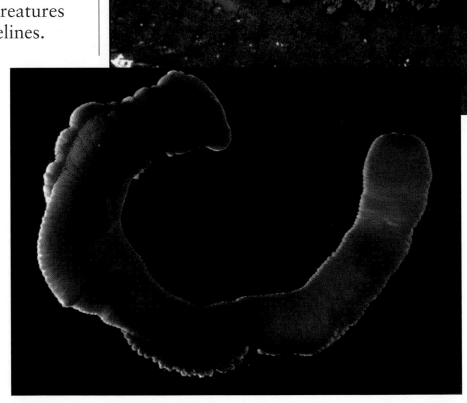

When is a worm not a worm? All worms belong to the supergroup of animals called invertebrates. Any creature with vertebrae—a backbone—cannot be a worm. Also any creature with proper limbs that have joints, like an insect's legs, is not a worm.

ACORN WORMS

There are several groups of creatures that almost break these guidelines. Acorn worms are soft-bodied, long, and plump. They live on the sea bed, some in U-shaped burrows, others under stones or among rocks. The largest are more than 6 feet (1.8 m) long. Their closest relatives, pterobranchs, are much smaller, and live in tubes joined together, like twigs on a tree.

Acorn worms and pterobranchs form the phylum Hemichordata, with about 80 species. Certain features inside the body, such as a hollow nerve cord along the top or dorsal side, mean that although they are invertebrates, they are cousins of fish and other vertebrates.

ACORN WORM
The acorn worm has a snoutlike proboscis. It feeds on tiny particles in the mud, as an earthworm eats soil.

DEFINITELY NOT WORMS

The huge arthropod group of animals includes insects, crabs and other crustaceans, spiders and scorpions, centipedes, and millipedes. Some of these, like millipedes, may look wormlike, but their limbs have proper joints and are not flexible all the way along. Many arthropods have a hard, rigid outer body casing, unlike the usually soft, moist covering of most worms.

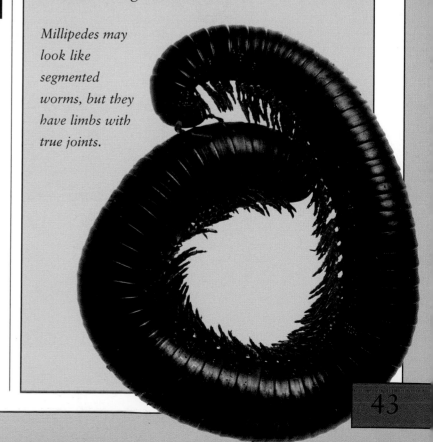

Millipedes may look like segmented worms, but they have limbs with true joints.

WALKING WORM

A velvet worm moves in a wormlike manner, making its body longer and shorter, as well as bending its fluid-filled "legs."

STUMPY "LEGS"

Velvet worms are slightly furry-looking and resemble caterpillars. There are about 70 species, forming the phylum Onychophora. Most live in tropical forests, among damp leaves, stones, and soil on the forest floor. Their "legs" are not true limbs with joints, but fleshy, bendy stumps, each tipped with two claws. There are usually between 20 and 40 pairs of "legs." These are true worms, but they are also close relatives of insects.

ANIMAL CLASSIFICATION

The animal kingdom can be split into two main groups, vertebrates (with a backbone) and invertebrates (without a backbone). From these two main groups, scientists classify, or sort, animals further based on their shared characteristics.

The six main groupings of animals, from the most general to the most specific, are: phylum, class, order, family, genus, and species. This system was created by Carolus Linnaeus.

To see how this system works, follow the example of how human beings are classified in the vertebrate group and how earthworms are classified in the invertebrate group.

ANIMAL KINGDOM

VERTEBRATE

PHYLUM: Chordata

CLASS: Mammals

ORDER: Primates

FAMILY: Hominids

GENUS: *Homo*

SPECIES: *sapiens*

INVERTEBRATE

PHYLUM: Annelida

CLASS: Oligochaeta

ORDER: Haplotaxida

FAMILY: Lumbricidae

GENUS: *Lumbricus*

SPECIES: *terrestris*

ANIMAL PHYLA

There are more than 30 groups of phyla. The nine most common are listed below along with their common name.

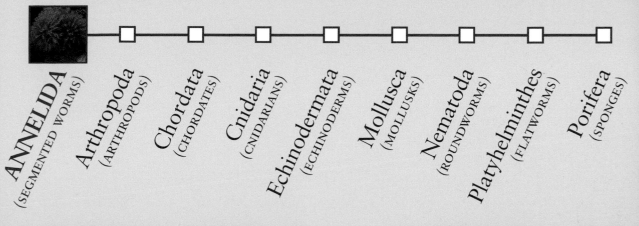

ANNELIDA
(SEGMENTED WORMS)

Arthropoda
(ARTHROPODS)

Chordata
(CHORDATES)

Cnidaria
(CNIDARIANS)

Echinodermata
(ECHINODERMS)

Mollusca
(MOLLUSKS)

Nematoda
(ROUNDWORMS)

Platyhelminthes
(FLATWORMS)

Porifera
(SPONGES)

This book highlights animals from the Annelida phylum. Follow the example below to learn how scientists classify the *Eudistylia polymorpha*, or the giant feather duster worm.

INVERTEBRATE

PHYLUM: Annelida

CLASS: Polychaeta

ORDER: Canalipalata

FAMILY: Sabellidae

GENUS: *Eudistylia*

SPECIES: *polymorpha*

Eudistylia polymorpha
(giant feather duster worm)

45

GLOSSARY

BIOLUMINESCENCE
When living things produce light and glow or flash, perhaps to lure prey or attract mates of their own kind for breeding

CARNIVORE
An animal that eats mainly other creatures, especially their flesh or meat

CILIA
Tiny short "hairs" that stick out from certain kinds of microscopic cells, and wave together like rows of miniature oars

COELOM
A fluid-filled chamber or cavity inside certain kinds of animals, including many types of worms

CUTICLE
The outer layer or "skin" of creatures such as worms, which is often thin, damp, and covered with mucus, or slime

EVERSIBLE
When something can be turned inside out

FOSSIL
The preserved remains of an animal or an impression in rock made by the body of an animal

HABITAT
A particular type of surroundings or environment where plants and animals live, such as a desert, pond, or seashore

HERBIVORE
An animal that eats mainly plant parts, including leaves, stems, fruits, and seeds

HERMAPHRODITE
Having both female and male breeding parts in the same body

INTROVERT
The headlike part of certain kinds of worms, into which the proboscis can be withdrawn

LARVA
The young, immature body form of some animals before it becomes an adult

LOPHOPHORE
A ring or "crown" of tentacles around the mouth in certain kinds of worms and other animals, used for feeding

PARAPODIA
Side extensions of the body segments, like flaps, which may be rounded or Y-shaped, as found in worms such as the ragworm

PARASITE
A living thing that gets a need such as food or shelter from another living thing, called the host, and harms the host in the process

PLANKTON
Tiny animals and other living organisms that live suspended in seawater

PROBOSCIS
An elongated snout or nose part, which is usually muscular and can bend; it is found in various animals, from the trunk of an elephant to the "snout" of worms

SEGMENT
A section or compartment of an animal's body, which is repeated many times; segments are especially obvious in the segmented worms or annelids

SETAE
Stiff hair or bristlelike structures found on the bodies of some animals, especially earthworms

TERRESTRIAL
Living mainly on land, on or in the ground, like earthworms that dwell in soil, or flatworms that live in the damp leaf litter of tropical rainforests

Look for more Animal Kingdom books:

Tree Frogs, Mud Puppies & Other Amphibians
ISBN 0-7565-1249-2

Ant Lions, Wasps & Other Insects
ISBN 0-7565-1250-6

Peacocks, Penguins & Other Birds
ISBN 0-7565-1251-4

Angelfish, Megamouth Sharks & Other Fish
ISBN 0-7565-1252-2

Bats, Blue Whales & Other Mammals
ISBN 0-7565-1249-2

Centipedes, Millipedes, Scorpions & Spiders
ISBN 0-7565-1254-9

Dwarf Geckos, Rattlesnakes & Other Reptiles
ISBN 0-7565-1255-7

Snails, Shellfish & Other Mollusks
ISBN 0-7565-1613-7

Lobsters, Crabs & Other Crustaceans
ISBN 0-7565-1612-9

Starfish, Urchins & Other Echinoderms
ISBN 0-7565-1611-0

Sponges, Jellyfish & Other Simple Animals
ISBN 0-7565-1614-5

FURTHER RESOURCES

AT THE LIBRARY
Blaxland, Beth. *Earthworms, Leeches, and Sea Worms: Annelids.* Philadelphia: Chelsea House Publishers, 2003.

Kalman, Bobbie. *The Life Cycle of an Earthworm.* New York: Crabtree Publishing, 2004.

Murray, Peter. *Worms.* Chanhassen, Minn.: Child's World, 2005.

Weber, Valerie. *Giant Tubeworms.* Milwaukee: Gareth Stevens Publishing, 2005.

ON THE WEB
For more information on *worms*, use FactHound to track down Web sites related to this book.
1.   Go to *www.facthound.com*
2.   Type in a search word related to this book or this book ID: 0756516153
3.   Click on the *Fetch It* button FactHound will find the best Web sites for you.

INDEX

A

Acanthocephala, 31
acorn worms, 42
annelids, 12, 18,
    19, 26
    leeches 17, 20
    polychaetes
    22, 25
arrowworms, 8,
    40, 41
Ascaris, 28

B

beard worms, 40
bioluminescence, 27
blood flukes, 32, 33
bloodworms, 12
bootlace worms,
    34-35
brandling
    worm, 14
breeding, 10, 12,
    18-19, 39
bristleworms, 22
Burgessochaeta, 13

C

cestodes, 33
chaetae, 25
Chaetognatha, 41
cocoon, 18, 19
coelom, 10
common bootlace
    worm, 34

D

deep-sea tube
    worms, 25
detritivores, 27
detritus worm, 12
digeans, 33

E

earthworms, 6, 9,
    10-11, 12, 26
    breeding 18, 19
    movement 16
    soil 14, 15
echiurans, 36, 37
eelworms, 28, 29
elephantiasis, 29
Enterobius, 29
eunice worm, 26

F

fan worms, 12, 17,
    24, 26
Fasciola, 33
filarial worms, 29
flatworms, 8, 32-33
flukes, 8, 32, 33

H

Hallucigenia, 13
Hemichordata, 42
hermaphrodite, 18
Hirudinea, 20
Hirudo medicinalis,
    21
hookworms, 29
horsehair worms,
    30-31
horseshoe worms, 39

K

keelworms, 25
king ragworm, 23

L

lancelet, 13
leeches, 12, 17, 18,
    19, 20-21
light sensors, 26
liver fluke, 33
lugworms, 8, 12, 22

M

mucus, 11, 18, 22,
    24, 37, 39
muscles, 10, 12, 16,
    17, 28

N

Nematomorpha, 30
Nemertea, 34
nematodes, 9, 28
nerves, 10, 11, 12,
    28, 32
Nippostrongylus,
    29

O

one-striped
    ribbonworm, 34
Onychophora, 43
Ottoia, 13

P

parapodia, 17
parasites, 8, 29, 30,
    31, 32, 33, 37
parchment worm,
    24
peacock worms, 24
peanut worms,
    8, 38
Phorona, 39
pig roundworm, 28
Pikaia, 13
pinworms, 29
planarians, 33
platyhelminths,
    32-33
Pogonophora, 40
polychaetes, 22,
    25, 27
priapulid worms
    13, 36-37
proboscis worms,
    35

P

proglottid, 33

R

ragworms, 12, 17,
    22, 23
ribbon worms, 8, 34
roundworms, 8, 9,
    34-35

S

sandworm, 23
scale worm, 25, 27
scarlet fanworm, 24
Schistosoma, 33
sea mouse, 25
segmented worms,
    10, 12
setae, 10, 12, 17
Sipuncula, 38
spaghetti worm, 27
spiny-headed
    worms, 30, 31
spoonworms,
    36, 37

T

tapeworms, 8,
    32, 33
theromyzon
    leech, 19
threadworms, 29
trematodes, 33
Trichostrongylus,
    28
tube worms 9,
    12, 25
turbellarians, 33

V

velvet worm, 43

W

Wucheria, 29